On Friday after school, Little Red Riding Hood Monster would leave the village to visit her monster grandmother who lived in a cottage in the middle of Once-Upon-a-Time Wood.

She always put on her red cloak and her mother and father would give her a hamper of things to take to her grandmother.

The hamper would have nice treats in it, such as bread and cakes, but also necessary things like flour, butter, shampoo, and soap. Little Red's mother would put a cover over the top to stop things falling out.

Little Red Riding Hood Monster would carry the hamper carefully so that she would not damage anything.

The woodland animals knew to listen out for Little Red's loud footsteps as she skipped (some might say stomped) along. They would scamper up into the trees, or hide, or keep right away from the track until she had gone by and it was safe again.

Little Red Riding Hood Monster was very kind and loved all the forest animals, but sometimes she just didn't see them as she stomped along, humming and swinging her hamper. She had sometimes stepped on an animal by mistake!

Everybody knew that Little Old Grandmother Monster lived alone in her cottage in the middle of Once-Upon-a-Time Wood, and that her lovely granddaughter visited her every Friday.
"She is such a lovely granddaughter!" they would say.

One day, somebody else was also in the woods. Big Bad overheard that a little old grandmother lived by herself in a cottage in the wood and had a hamper of lovely things delivered to her every Friday.

"I will deal with the frail old grandmother, and then I will have a hamper of lovely things delivered to ME every Friday!" he chuckled.

Big Bad was very happy with his plan, and he jumped happily around in a circle singing, "I'm so clever. I'm so clever!"

He smiled slyly and then continued humming as he slunk along. He crept from tree to tree in the forest, keeping to the shadows as he made his way to Grandmother Monster's little cottage.

When Big Bad got close to Grandmother Monster's cottage, he hid, and then peered around to check if anybody was there. He slid to the next tree and looked again, and then he edged closer. Still he couldn't see anyone.

Elsewhere in the wood, Little Red Riding Hood Monster was stamping along in her big red cloak. Her hood was so big that it always fell and covered her face.

"Hello!" called (or bellowed) Little Red to the animals. "Hello squirrels! Hello birds!" she boomed, and waved at them as they safely perched in the trees.

“Hello! How is your grandmother?” called Mother Badger from the doorway of the sett where she lived.

“I’m afraid she hasn’t been very well,” replied Little Red. “Mother phoned her this morning and now I’m taking her some lemons and medicine.”

"Oh dear! Send her my love," said Mother Badger. "I will," replied (or yelled) Little Red as she continued on her way.

After she had gone, the badger cubs were allowed back out to play, the rabbit kits emerged from their burrow, and the squirrels scampered back down from the tops of the trees.

Meanwhile, back at Grandmother Monster's cottage, Big Bad was squinting in at the kitchen window. The kitchen was empty, but in the sitting room beyond he could see Grandmother Monster wrapped in a tartan blanket, with a white mop cap covering her head. She was sound asleep on the couch and snoring thunderously.

The door opened with a gentle "snick" sound, and a silver shadow slipped noiselessly into the cottage. Big Bad licked his lips and smiled as he looked at the sleeping, frail, little old grandmother.

"This is going to be so easy," he murmured. "First, Little Old Grandmother Monster, and then a whole hamper of treats. I cannot wait!"

In the sitting room, Grandmother Monster had heard the faint "snick" of the door knob, and the careful steps approaching her. She opened one eye a little and listened as the footsteps got closer and closer.

As Big Bad got to the edge of the couch, Grandmother Monster could see him getting ready to pounce. Suddenly, she whipped up and spun around, in a swirl of tartan shawl and fur, with flashing eyes and very long, sharp, pointed teeth.

A couple of snaps of those sharp, pointed teeth and Grandmother Monster was once again alone in the little cottage!

“Hello, Granny! Yoo-hoo!” called Little Red Riding Hood Monster as she arrived at the cottage. She took off her cloak and hung it on a hook by the door.

“Father has put some cold medicine in the hamper for you today, and some fresh lemons. There are also some of the cinnamon buns we made yesterday, plus the other things you said you needed.”

The two monsters sat and enjoyed a cup of tea with a cinnamon bun.
Grandmother Monster suddenly burped. She rubbed her tummy and then burped loudly again. "Pardon me," she said. "I must have eaten something that didn't agree with me!" she chuckled and winked.